HORRID HENRY

AND THE
SCARY SITTER

Meet HORRID HENRY
the laugh-out-loud worldwide sensation!

....

* Over 15 million copies sold in 27 countries and counting

* # 1 chapter book series in the UK

* Francesca Simon is the only American author to ever win the Galaxy British Book Awards Children's Book of the year (past winners include J.K. Rowling, Philip Pullman, and Eoin Colfer).

"Horrid Henry is a fabulous antihero…**a modern comic classic**." —*Guardian*

"**Wonderfully appealing to girls and boys alike**, a precious rarity at this age." —Judith Woods, *Times*

. . . .

"The best children's comic writer." —Amanda Craig, Times

. . . .

"**I love the Horrid Henry books by Francesca Simon**. They have lots of funny bits in. And Henry always gets into trouble!" —Mia, age 6, *BBC Learning Is Fun*

"My two boys love this book, and **I have actually had tears running down my face and had to stop reading because of laughing so hard**." —T. Franklin, Parent

"**It's easy to see why Horrid Henry is the bestselling character for five- to eight-year-olds**." —*Liverpool Echo*

"Francesca Simon's truly horrific little boy is **a monstrously enjoyable creation**. Parents love them because Henry makes their own little darlings seem like angels." —*Guardian Children's Books Supplement*

"I have tried out the Horrid Henry books with groups of children as a parent, as a babysitter, and as a teacher. **Children love to either hear them read aloud or to read them themselves**." —Danielle Hall, Teacher

"A flicker of recognition must pass through most teachers and parents when they read Horrid Henry. **There's a tiny bit of him in all of us**." —Nancy Astee, *Child Education*

"**As a teacher…it's great to get a series of books my class loves**. They go mad for Horrid Henry." —A teacher

"**Henry is a beguiling hero who has entranced millions of reluctant readers**." —*Herald*

"AN absolutely fantastic series and surely a winner with all children. Long live Francesca Simon and her brilliant books! More, more please!" —A parent

"**Laugh-out-loud reading for both adults and children alike**." —A parent

"**Horrid Henry certainly lives up to his name, and his antics are everything you hope your own child will avoid—which is precisely why younger children so enjoy these tales**." —*Independent on Sunday*

"Henry might be unbelievably naughty, totally wicked, and utterly horrid, but **he is frequently credited with converting the most reluctant readers into enthusiastic ones**…superb in its simplicity." —*Liverpool Echo*

Horrid Henry by Francesca Simon

HORRID HENRY

AND THE
SCARY SITTER

Francesca Simon
Illustrated by Tony Ross

sourcebooks
young readers

Published by Sourcebooks Young Readers, an imprint of Sourcebooks Kids
P.O. Box 4410, Naperville, Illinois 60567-4410
(630) 961-3900
sourcebookskids.com

Originally published in Great Britain in 2002 by Orion Children's Books.

Library of Congress Cataloging-in-Publication Data

Simon, Francesca.
  Horrid Henry and the scary sitter / Francesca
Simon ; illustrated by Tony Ross.
      v. cm.
  Contents: Horrid Henry tricks and treats—Horrid Henry and the
bogey babysitter—Horrid Henry's raid—Horrid Henry's car journey.
  [1. Behavior—Fiction.] I. Ross, Tony, ill. II. Title.
  PZ7.S604Hre 2009
  [Fic]—dc22
2009017470

Source of Production: Berryville Graphics Inc., Berryville, Virginia, United States
Date of Production: October 2019
Run Number: 5016857

Printed and bound in the United States of America.
BVG   10 9 8 7 6 5 4 3 2 1

*To my old friends Caroline Elton and
Andrew Franklin, and my new ones
Miriam, Jonathan, and Michael*

CONTENTS

1

HORRID HENRY TRICKS AND TREATS

Halloween! Oh happy, happy day! Every year Horrid Henry could not believe it: an entire day devoted to stuffing your face with candy and playing horrid tricks. Best of all, you were *supposed* to stuff your face and play horrid tricks. Whoopee!

Horrid Henry was armed and ready. He had toilet paper rolls. He had water pistols. He had shaving cream. Oh my, would he be playing tricks tonight. Anyone who didn't instantly hand over a fistful of candy would get it with the cream. And woe betide any fool who gave him an apple. Horrid Henry knew how to treat rotten grown-ups like that.

His red and black devil costume lay ready on the bed, complete with evil mask, twinkling horns, trident, and whippy tail. He'd scare everyone wearing that.

"Heh heh heh," said Horrid Henry, practicing his evil laugh.

"Henry," came a little voice outside his bedroom door, "come and see my new costume."

"No," said Henry.

"Oh please, Henry," said his younger brother, Perfect Peter.

"No," said Henry. "I'm busy."

"You're just jealous because *my* costume is nicer than yours," said Peter.

"Am not."

"Are too."

Come to think of it, what *was* Peter wearing? Last year he'd copied Henry's monster costume and ruined Henry's

2

Halloween. What if he were copying Henry's devil costume? That would be just like that horrible little copycat.

"All right, you can come in for two seconds," said Henry.

A big, pink, bouncy bunny bounded into Henry's room. It had little white bunny ears. It had a little white bunny tail. It had pink polka dots everywhere else. Horrid Henry groaned. What a stupid costume. Thank goodness *he* wasn't wearing it.

"Isn't it great?" said Perfect Peter.

"No," said Henry. "It's horrible."

"You're just saying that to be mean, Henry," said Peter, bouncing up and down. "I can't wait to go trick-or-treating in it tonight."

Oh no. Horrid Henry felt as if he'd been punched in the stomach. Henry would be expected to go out trick-or-treating—with Peter! He, Henry, would have to walk around with a pink polka dot bunny. Everyone would see him. The shame of it! Rude Ralph would never stop teasing him. Moody Margaret would call him a bunny wunny. How could he play tricks on people with a pink polka dot bunny following him everywhere? He was ruined. His name would be a joke.

"You can't wear that," said Henry desperately.

"Yes I can," said Peter.

4

"I won't let you," said Henry.

Perfect Peter looked at Henry. "You're just jealous."

Grrr! Horrid Henry was about to tear that stupid costume off Peter when, suddenly, he had an idea.

It was painful.

It was humiliating.

But anything was better than having Peter prancing about in pink polka dots.

"Tell you what," said Henry, "just because I'm so nice I'll let you borrow my monster costume. You've always wanted to wear it."

"NO!" said Peter. "I want to be a bunny."

"But you're supposed to be scary for Halloween," said Henry.

"I am scary," said Peter. "I'm going to bounce up to people and yell 'boo'."

"I can make you really scary, Peter," said Horrid Henry.

"How?" said Peter.

"Sit down and I'll show you." Henry patted his desk chair.

"What are you going to do?" said Peter suspiciously. He took a step back.

"Nothing," said Henry. "I'm just trying to help you."

Perfect Peter didn't move.

"How can I be scarier?" he said cautiously.

"I can give you a scary haircut," said Henry.

Perfect Peter clutched his curls.

"But I like my hair," he said feebly.

"This is Halloween," said Henry. "Do you want to be scary or don't you?"

"Um, um, uh," said Peter, as Henry pushed him down in the chair and got out the scissors.

"Not too much," squealed Peter.

"Of course not," said Horrid Henry. "Just sit back and relax, I promise you'll love this."

Horrid Henry twirled the scissors.

Snip! Snip! Snip! Snip! Snip!

Magnificent, thought Horrid Henry. He gazed proudly at his work. Maybe he should be a hairdresser when he grew up. Yes! Henry could see it now. Customers would line up for miles for one of Monsieur Henri's scary snips. Shame his genius was wasted on someone as yucky as Peter. Still…

"You look great, Peter," said Henry. "Really scary. Atomic Bunny. Go and have a look."

Peter went over and looked in the mirror.

"AAAAAAAAAARGGGGGGG!"

"Scared yourself, did you?" said Henry. "That's great."

"AAAAAAAAAARGGGGGGG!" howled Peter.

Mom ran into the room.

"AAAAAAAAAARGGGGGGG!" howled Mom.

"AAAAAAAAAARGGGGGGG!" howled Peter.

"Henry!" screeched Mom. "What have you done?! You horrid, horrid boy!"

What was left of Peter's hair stuck up in ragged tufts all over his head. On one side was a big bald patch.

"I was just making

8

him look scary," pro-
tested Henry. "He
said I could."

"Henry made
me!" said Peter.

"My poor baby," said
Mom. She glared at Henry.

"No trick-or-treating for you,"
said Mom. "You'll stay here."

Horrid Henry could hardly believe his
ears. This was the worst thing that had
ever happened to him.

"NO!" howled Henry. This was all
Peter's fault.

"I hate you Peter!" he screeched.
Then he attacked. He was Medusa, coil-
ing around her victim with her snaky
hair.

"Aaaahh!" screeched Peter.

"Henry!" shouted Mom. "Go to your
room!"

Mom and Peter left the house to go
trick-or-treating. Henry had screamed
and sobbed and begged. He'd put on
his devil costume, just in case his tears
melted their stony hearts. But no. His
mean, horrible parents wouldn't change
their minds. Well, they'd be sorry.
They'd all be sorry.

Dad came into the living room. He
was holding a large shopping bag.

"Henry, I've got some work to finish
so I'm going to let you hand out treats
to any trick-or-treaters."

Horrid Henry stopped plotting his
revenge. Had Dad gone crazy? Hand out

treats? What kind of
punishment was this?

Horrid Henry
fought to keep a big
smile off his face.

"Here's the
Halloween stuff,

Henry," said Dad. He handed Henry the
heavy bag. "But remember," he added
sternly, "these treats are not for you:
they're to give away."

Yeah, right, thought Henry.

"OK, Dad," he said as meekly as he
could. "Whatever you say."

Dad went back to the kitchen. Now
was his chance! Horrid Henry leapt on
the bag. Wow, was it full! He'd grab
all the good stuff, throw back anything
yucky with lime or peppermint, and
he'd have enough candy to keep him
going for at least a week!

Henry yanked open the bag. A terri-
ble sight met his eyes. The bag was full

11

of oranges. And apples. And walnuts
in their shells. No wonder his horrible
parents had trusted him to be in charge
of it.

Ding dong.

Slowly, Horrid Henry heaved his
heavy bones to the door. There was his
empty, useless trick-or-treat bag, sitting
forlornly by the entrance. Henry gave it
a kick, then opened the door and glared.

"Whaddya want?"
snapped Horrid Henry.

"Trick-or-treat,"
whispered Weepy
William. He was
dressed as a pirate.

Horrid Henry held
out the bag of horrors.

"Grab bag!" he
announced. "Close
your eyes for a big
surprise!"

12

William certainly
would be surprised at
what a rotten treat
he'd be getting.

Weepy William put
down his swag bag, closed
his eyes tight, then plunged his hand
into Henry's grab bag. He rummaged and
he rummaged and he rummaged, hoping
to find something better than oranges.

Horrid Henry eyed Weepy William's
bulging swag bag.

Go on Henry, urged the bag. He'll
never notice.

Horrid Henry did not wait to be asked
twice.

Dip!

Zip!

Pop!

Horrid Henry grabbed a big handful of
William's candy and popped them inside
his empty bag.

13

Weepy William opened his eyes.

"Did you take some of my candy?"

"No," said Henry.

William peeked inside his bag and burst into tears.

"Waaaaaaaa!" wailed William. "Henry took—"

Henry pushed him out and slammed the door.

Dad came running.

"What's wrong?"

"Nothing," said Henry. "Just William crying 'cause he's scared of pumpkins."

Phew, thought Henry. That was close. Perhaps he had been a little too greedy.

Ding dong.

It was Lazy Linda wearing a pillowcase over her head. Gorgeous Gurinder was with her, dressed as a scarecrow.

14

"Trick-or-treat!"

"Trick-or-treat!"

"Close your eyes
for a big surprise!"
said Henry, holding
out the grab bag.

"Ooh, a grab bag!"
squealed Linda.

Lazy Linda and Gorgeous Gurinder put
down their bags, closed their eyes, and
reached into the grab bag.

Dip!

Zip!

Pop!

Dip!

Zip!

Pop!

Lazy Linda opened her eyes.

"You give the worst treats ever, Henry,"
said Linda, gazing at her walnut in disgust.

"We won't be coming back *here*,"
sniffed Gorgeous Gurinder.

Tee hee, thought Horrid Henry.

Ding dong.

It was Beefy Bert. He was wearing a robot costume.

"Hi Bert, got any good candy?" asked Henry.

"I dunno," said Beefy Bert.

Horrid Henry soon found out that he did. Lots and lots and lots. So did Moody Margaret, Sour Susan, Jolly Josh, and Tidy Ted. Soon Henry's bag was stuffed with treats.

Ding dong.

Horrid Henry opened the door.

"Boo," said Atomic Bunny.

Henry's candy bag! Help! Mom would see it!

"Eeeeek!" screeched
Horrid Henry. "Help!
Save me!"

Quickly, he ran
upstairs clutching his
bag and hid it safely
under his bed. Phew,
that was close.

"Don't be scared, Henry, it's only
me," called Perfect Peter.

Horrid Henry came back downstairs.

"No!" said Henry. "I'd never have
known."

"Really?" said Peter.

"Really," said Henry.

"Everyone just gave candy this year,"
said Perfect Peter. "Yuck."

Horrid Henry held out the grab bag.

"Ooh, an orange," said Peter. "Aren't
I lucky!"

"I hope you've learned your lesson,
Henry," said Mom sternly.

"I certainly have," said Horrid Henry,
eyeing Perfect Peter's bulging bag.
"Good things come to those who wait."

2

HORRID HENRY AND THE SCARY SITTER

"No way!" shrieked Tetchy Tess, slamming down the phone.

"No way!" shrieked Crabby Chris, slamming down the phone.

"No way!" shrieked Angry Anna. "What do you think I am, crazy?"

Even Mellow Martin said he was busy.

Mom hung up the phone and groaned.

It wasn't easy finding someone to babysit more than once for Horrid Henry. When Tetchy Tess came, Henry flooded the bathroom. When Crabby Chris came he hid her homework and "accidentally" poured red grape juice down the front of her new white jeans. And when Angry Anna came, Henry— no, it's too dreadful. Suffice it to say that Anna ran screaming from the house and Henry's parents had to come home early.

Horrid Henry hated babysitters. He wasn't a baby. He didn't want to be sat on. Why should he be nice to some ugly, stuck-up, bossy teenager who'd hog the TV and pig out on Henry's cookies? Parents should just stay at home where they belonged, thought Horrid Henry.

And now it looked like they would have to. Ha! His parents were mean and horrible, but he'd had a lot of practice managing them. Babysitters were unpredictable. Babysitters were hard work. And by the time you'd broken them in and shown them who was boss, for some reason they didn't want to come any more. The only good babysitters let you stay

up all night and eat candy until you were
sick. Sadly, Horrid Henry never got one
of those.

"We have to find a babysitter," wailed
Mom. "The party is tomorrow night.
I've tried everyone. Who else is there?"

"There's got to be someone," said
Dad. "Think!"

Mom thought.

Dad thought.

"What about Rebecca?" said Dad.

Horrid Henry's heart missed a beat. He
stopped drawing mustaches on Perfect
Peter's school pictures. Maybe he'd

heard wrong. Oh please, not Rebecca!
Not—Rabid Rebecca!

"Who did you say?" asked Henry. His
voice quavered.

"You heard me," said Dad. "Rebecca."

"NO!" screamed Henry. "She's
horrible!"

"She's not horrible," said Dad. "She's
just—strict."

"There's no one else," said Mom
grimly. "I'll call Rebecca."

"She's a monster!" wailed Henry. "She
made Ralph go to bed at six o'clock!"

"I like going to bed at six o'clock," said
Perfect Peter. "After all, growing children
need their rest."

Horrid Henry growled and attacked.
He was the Creature from the Black

Lagoon, dragging the foolish mortal
down to a watery grave.

"AAAEEEEE!" squealed Peter. "Henry
pulled my hair."

"Stop being horrid, Henry!" said Dad.
"Mom's on the phone."

Henry prayed. Maybe she'd be busy.
Maybe she'd say no. Maybe she'd be dead.
He'd heard all about Rebecca. She'd made
Tough Toby get in his pajamas at five
o'clock *and* do all his homework. She'd
unplugged Dizzy Dave's computer. She'd

25

made Moody Margaret wash the floor. No doubt about it, Rabid Rebecca was the toughest teen in town.

Henry lay on the rug and howled. Mom shouted into the phone.

"You can! That's great, Rebecca. No, that's just the TV—sorry for the noise. See you tomorrow."

"NOOOOOOOOO!" wailed Henry.

Ding dong.

"I'll get it!" said Perfect Peter. He skipped to the door.

Henry flung himself on the carpet.

"I DON'T WANT TO HAVE A BABYSITTER!" he wailed.

The door opened. In walked the biggest, meanest, ugliest, nastiest-looking girl Henry had ever seen. Her arms were enormous. Her head was enormous. Her teeth were enormous. She looked like she ate elephants for breakfast,

crocodiles for lunch, and snacked on toddlers.

"What have you got to eat?" snarled Rabid Rebecca.

Dad took a step back. "Help yourself to anything in the fridge," said Dad.

"Don't worry, I will," said Rebecca.

"GO HOME, YOU WITCH!" howled Henry.

"Bedtime is nine o'clock," shouted Dad, trying to be heard above Henry's screams. He edged his way carefully past Rebecca, jumped over Henry, then dashed out the front door.

"I DON'T WANT TO HAVE A BABYSITTER!" shrieked Henry.

"Be good, Henry," said Mom weakly. She stepped over Henry, then escaped from the house.

The door closed.

Horrid Henry was alone in the house with Rabid Rebecca.

He glared at Rebecca.

Rebecca glared at him.

"I've heard all about you, you little creep," growled Rebecca. "No one bothers me when I'm babysitting."

Horrid Henry stopped screaming.

"Oh yeah," said Horrid Henry. "We'll see about that."

Rabid Rebecca bared her fangs. Henry recoiled. Perhaps I'd better keep out of her way, he thought, then slipped into the living room and turned on the TV.

Ahh, Mutant Max. Hurray! How bad could life be when a great program like Mutant Max was on? He'd annoy Rebecca as soon as it was over.

Rebecca stomped into the room and snatched the remote.

ZAP!

DA DOO, DA DOO DA, DA DOO DA DOO DA, tangoed some horrible spangled dancers.

"Hey," said Henry. "I'm watching Mutant Max."

"Tough," said Rebecca. "*I'm* watching ballroom dancing."

Snatch!

Horrid Henry grabbed the clicker.

ZAP!

"And it's mutants, mutants, mut—"

Snatch!

Zap!

31

DA DOO, DA DOO DA, DA DOO DA DOO DA.

DOO, DA DOO DA, DA DOO DA DOO DA.

Horrid Henry tangoed around the room, gliding and sliding.

"Stop it," muttered Rebecca.

Henry shimmied back and forth in front of the TV, blocking her view and singing along as loudly as he could.

"DA DOO, DA DOO DA," warbled Henry.

"I'm warning you," hissed Rebecca.

Perfect Peter walked in. He had already put on his blue bunny pajamas, brushed his teeth, and combed his hair. He held a game of Chinese Checkers in his hand.

"Rebecca, will you play a game with me before I go to bed?" asked Peter.

"NO!" roared Rebecca. "I'm trying to watch TV. Shut up and go away."

Perfect Peter leapt back.

"But I thought—since I was all ready for bed—" he stammered.

"I've got better things to do than to play with you," snarled Rebecca. "Now go to bed this minute, both of you."

"But it's not my bedtime for hours," protested Henry. "I want to watch Mutant Max."

"Or mine," said Perfect Peter timidly. "There's this nature program—"

"GO!" howled Rebecca.

"NO!" howled Henry.

"RAAAAA!" roared Rabid Rebecca.

Horrid Henry did not know how it happened. It was as if fiery dragon's breath had blasted him upstairs. Somehow, he was

34

in his pajamas, in bed, and it was only
seven o'clock.

Rabid Rebecca switched off the light.
"Don't even think of moving from that
bed," she hissed. "If I see you, or hear
you, or even smell you, you'll be sorry
you were born. I'll stay
downstairs, you stay
upstairs, and that
way no one will
get hurt." Then she
marched out of the
room and slammed
the door.

Horrid Henry was so shocked he
could not move. He, Horrid Henry,
the bulldozer of babysitters, the terror
of teachers, the bully of brothers, was in
bed, lights out, at seven o'clock.

Seven o'clock! Two whole hours
before his bedtime! This was an outrage!
He could hear Moody Margaret shrieking

next door. He could hear Toddler Tom
zooming around on his tricycle. No one
went to bed at seven o'clock. Not even
toddlers!

Worst of all, he was thirsty. So what
if she told me to stay in bed, thought
Horrid Henry. I'm thirsty. I'm going to
go downstairs and get myself a glass of
water. It's my house and I'll do what I
want.

Horrid Henry did not move.

I'm dying of thirst here, thought
Henry. Mom and Dad will come home

and I'll be a dried out old stick insect,
and boy will she be in trouble.

Horrid Henry still did not move.

Go on, feet, urged Henry, let's just step
on down and get a little ol' glass of water.
So what if that scary sitter said he had to
stay in bed. What could
she do to him?

She could chop
off my head and
bounce it down
the stairs, thought
Henry.

Eeek.

Well, let her
try.

Horrid Henry remembered who he
was. The boy who'd sent teachers shriek-
ing from the classroom. The boy who'd
destroyed the Demon Dinner Lady. The
boy who had run away from home and
almost reached the Congo.

I will get up and get a drink of water,
he thought.

Sneak. Sneak. Sneak.

Horrid Henry crept to the bedroom
door.

Slowly he opened it a crack.

Creak.
Then slowly,
slowly, he opened
the door a bit more
and slipped out.
ARGHHHHHH!

There was Rabid Rebecca sitting at
the top of the stairs.

It's a trap, thought Henry. She was lying
in wait for me. I'm dead, I'm finished,
they'll find my bones in the morning.

Horrid Henry dashed back inside his
room and awaited his doom.

Silence.

What was going on? Why hadn't
Rebecca torn him apart limb from limb?

Horrid Henry opened his door a fraction and peeped out.

Rabid Rebecca was still sitting huddled at the top of the stairs. She did not move. Her eyes were fixed straight ahead.

"Spi–spi–spider," she whispered. She pointed at a big, hairy spider in front of her with a trembling hand.

"It's huge," said Henry. "Really hairy and horrible and wriggly and—"

"STOP!" squealed Rebecca. "Help me, Henry," she begged.

Horrid Henry was not the fearless leader of a pirate gang for nothing.

"If I risk my life and get rid of the spider, can I watch Mutant Max?" asked Henry.

"Yes," said Rebecca.

"And stay up 'til my parents come home?"

"Yes," said Rebecca.

"And eat all the ice cream in the fridge?"

"YES!" shrieked Rebecca. "Just get rid of that—that—"

"Deal," said Horrid Henry.

He dashed to his room and grabbed a jar.

Rabid Rebecca hid her eyes as Horrid Henry scooped up the spider. What a beauty!

"It's gone," said Henry.

Rebecca opened her beady red eyes.

"Right, back to bed, you little brat!"

"What?" said Henry.

"Bed. Now!" screeched Rebecca.

"But we agreed…" said Henry.

"Tough," said Rebecca. "That was then."

"Traitor," said Henry.

He whipped out the spider jar from behind his back and unscrewed the lid.

"On guard!" he said.

"AAEEEE!" whimpered Rebecca.

Horrid Henry advanced menacingly toward her.

"NOOOOOOO!" wailed Rebecca, stepping back.

"Now get in that room and stay there," ordered Henry. "Or else."

Rabid Rebecca skedaddled into the bathroom and locked the door.

"If I see you or hear you or even smell you, you'll be sorry you were born," said Henry.

"I already am," said Rabid Rebecca.

Horrid Henry spent a lovely evening in front of the TV. He watched scary movies. He ate ice cream and candy and cookies and chips until he could stuff no more in.

Vroom vroom.

Oops. Parents home.

Horrid Henry dashed upstairs and leapt into bed just as the front door opened.

Mom and Dad looked around the living room, littered with candy wrappers, cookie crumbs, and ice cream cartons.

"You did tell her to help herself," said Mom.

"Still," said Dad. "What a pig."

"Never mind," said Mom brightly, "at least she managed to get Henry to bed. That's a first."

Rabid Rebecca staggered into the room.

"Did you get enough to eat?" said Dad.

"No," said Rabid Rebecca.

"Oh," said Dad.

"Was everything all right?" asked Mom.

Rebecca looked at her.

"Can I go now?" said Rebecca.

"Any chance you could babysit on Saturday?" asked Dad hopefully.

"What do you think I am, crazy?" shrieked Rebecca.

SLAM!

Upstairs, Horrid Henry groaned.

Rats. It was so unfair. Just when he had a babysitter beautifully trained, for some reason they wouldn't come back.

3

HORRID HENRY'S RAID

"You're such a pig, Susan!"

"No I'm not! You're the pig!"

"You are!" squealed Moody Margaret.

"You are!" squealed Sour Susan.

"Oink!"

"Oink!"

All was not well at Moody Margaret's Secret Club.

Sour Susan and Moody Margaret glared at each other inside the Secret Club tent. Moody Margaret waved the empty cookie tin in Susan's sour face.

"*Someone* ate all the cookies," said Moody Margaret. "And it wasn't me."

"Well, it wasn't me," said Susan.

"Liar!"

"Liar!"

Margaret stuck out her tongue at Susan.
Susan stuck out her tongue at Margaret.
Margaret yanked Susan's hair.

"Oww! You horrible meanie!"
shrieked Susan. "I hate you."

She yanked Margaret's hair.

"OWWW!" screeched Moody
Margaret. "How dare you?"

They scowled at each other.

"Wait a minute," said Margaret. "You
don't think—"

★ ★ ★

Not a million miles
away, sitting on a
throne inside the
Purple Hand fort
hidden behind
prickly branches,
Horrid Henry wiped

a few cookie crumbs from his mouth
and burped. Mmmm boy, nothing beat
the taste of an archenemy's cookies.

The branches parted.

"Password!" hissed Horrid Henry.

"Smelly toads."

"Enter," said Henry.

The guard entered and gave the secret
handshake.

"Henry, why—" began Perfect Peter.

"Call me by my title, Worm!"

"Sorry, Henry—I mean Lord High
Excellent Majesty of the Purple Hand."

"That's better," said Henry. He waved
his hand and pointed at the ground. "Be
seated, Worm."

"Why am I Worm and you're Lord High Excellent Majesty?"

"Because I'm the leader," said Henry.

"I want a better title," said Peter.

"All right," said the Lord High Excellent Majesty, "you can be Lord Worm."

Peter considered.

"What about Lord High Worm?"

"OK," said Henry. Then he froze.

"Worm! Footsteps!"

Perfect Peter peeked through the leaves.

"Enemies approaching!" he warned.

Pounding feet paused outside the entrance.

"Password!" said Horrid Henry.

"Dog poo breath," said Margaret, bursting in. Sour Susan followed.

"That's not the password," said Henry.

"You can't come in," squeaked the guard, a little late.

"You've been stealing the Secret Club cookies," said Moody Margaret.

"Yeah, Henry," said Susan.

Horrid Henry stretched and yawned.

"Prove it."

Moody Margaret pointed to all the crumbs lying on the dirt floor.

"Where did all these crumbs come from, then?"

"Cookies," said Henry.

"So you admit it!" shrieked Margaret.

"Purple Hand cookies," said Henry. He pointed to the Purple Hand skull

and crossbones cookie tin.

"Liar, liar, pants on fire," said Margaret.

Horrid Henry fell to the floor and started rolling around.

"Ooh, ooh, my pants are on fire, I'm burning, call the fire fighters!" shouted Henry.

Perfect Peter dashed off.

"Mom!" he hollered. "Henry's pants are on fire!"

Margaret and Susan made a hasty retreat. Horrid Henry stopped rolling and howled with laughter.

52

"Ha ha ha ha ha—the Purple Hand rules!" he cackled.

"We'll get you for this, Henry," said Margaret.

"Yeah, yeah," said Henry.

"You didn't really steal their cookies, did you, Henry?" asked Lord High Worm the following day.

"As if," said Horrid Henry. "Now get back to your guard duty. Our enemies may be planning a revenge attack."

"Why do I always have to be the guard?" said Peter. "It's not fair."

"Whose club is this?" said Henry fiercely.

Peter's lip began to tremble.

"Yours," muttered Peter.

"So if you want to stay as a temporary member, you have to do what I say," said Henry.

"OK," said Peter.

"And remember, one day, if you're

very good, you'll be promoted from junior guard to chief guard," said Henry.

"Ooh," said Peter, brightening.

Business settled, Horrid Henry reached for the cookie tin. He'd saved five yummy chocolate fudge chewies for today.

Henry picked up the tin and stopped. Why wasn't it rattling? He shook it.

Silence.

Horrid Henry ripped off the lid and shrieked.

The Purple Hand cookie tin was empty. Except for one thing. A dagger drawn on a piece of paper. The dastardly mark of Margaret's Secret Club! Well, he'd show them who ruled.

"Worm!" he shrieked. "Get in here!"

Peter entered.

"We've been raided!" screamed Henry. "You're fired!"

"Waaaah!" wailed Peter.

★ ★ ★

"Good work, Susan," said the leader of the Secret Club, her face covered in chocolate.

"I don't see why you got three cookies and I only got two when I was the one who sneaked in and stole them," said Susan sourly.

"Tribute to your leader," said Moody Margaret.

"I still don't think it's fair," muttered Susan.

"Tough," said Margaret. "Now let's hear your spy report."

"NAH NAH NE NAH NAH!" screeched a voice from outside.

Susan and Margaret dashed out of the Secret Club tent. They were too late. There was Henry, prancing off, waving the Secret Club banner he'd stolen.

"Give that back, Henry!" screamed Margaret.

"Make me!" said Henry.

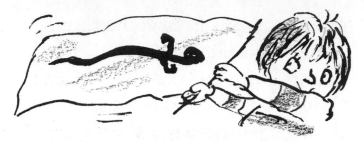

Susan chased him. Henry darted.
Margaret chased him. Henry dodged.
"Come and get me!" taunted Henry.
"All right," said Margaret. She walked
toward him, then suddenly jumped over
the wall into Henry's garden and ran to
the Purple Hand fort.

"Hey, get away from there!" shouted
Henry, chasing after her. Where was that
useless guard when you needed him?

Margaret nabbed Henry's skull and
crossbones flag and darted off.

The two leaders faced each other.

"Gimme my flag!" ordered Henry.

"Gimme my flag!" ordered Margaret.

"You first," said Henry.

"*You* first," said Margaret.

Neither moved.

"OK, at the count of three we'll throw them to each other," said Margaret.

One, two, three—throw!"

Margaret held on to Henry's flag.

Henry held on to Margaret's flag.

Several moments passed.

"Cheater," said Margaret.

"Cheater," said Henry.

"I don't know about you, but I have important spying work to get on with," said Margaret.

"So?" said Henry. "Get on with it. No one's stopping you."

"Drop my flag, Henry," said Margaret.

"No," said Henry.

"Fine," said Margaret. "Susan! Bring me the scissors."

Susan ran off.

"Peter!" shouted Henry. "Worm! Lord Worm! Lord High Worm!"

Peter stuck his head out of the upstairs window.

"Peter! Get the scissors! Quick!" ordered Henry.

"No," said Peter. "You fired me, remember?" And he slammed the window shut.

"You're dead, Peter," shouted Henry.

Sour Susan came back with the scissors
and gave them to Margaret. Margaret
held the scissors to Henry's flag. Henry
didn't budge. She wouldn't dare—

Snip!

Aaargh! Moody Margaret cut off a
corner of Henry's flag. She held the
scissors poised to make another cut.

Horrid Henry had spent hours painting
his beautiful flag. He knew when he was
beat.

"Stop!" shrieked Henry.

He dropped Margaret's flag. Margaret
dropped his flag. Slowly, they inched
toward each other, then dashed to grab
their own flag.

"Truce?" said Moody Margaret, beaming.

"Truce," said Horrid Henry, scowling.

I'll get her for this, thought Horrid Henry. No one touches my flag and lives.

Horrid Henry watched and waited until it was dark and he heard the plinky-plonk sound of Moody Margaret practicing her piano.

The coast was clear. Horrid Henry sneaked outside, jumped over the wall and darted inside the Secret Club Tent.

Swoop! He swept up the Secret Club pencils and secret code book.

Snatch! He snaffled the Secret Club stool.

Grab! He bagged the Secret Club cookie tin.

Was that everything?

No!

Scoop! He snatched the Secret Club motto ("Down with boys").

Pounce! He stole the Secret Club carpet.

Horrid Henry looked around. The Secret Club tent was bare.

Except for—

Henry considered. Should he?

Yes!

Whisk! The Secret Club tent collapsed.

Henry gathered it into his arms with the rest of his spoils.

Huffing and puffing, gasping and panting, Horrid Henry staggered off over the wall, laden with the Secret Club.

Raiding was hot, heavy work, but a pirate had to do his duty. Wouldn't all this booty look great decorating his fort? A rug on the floor, an extra cookie tin, a repainted motto—"Down with girls"— yes, the Purple Hand Fort would have to be renamed the Purple Hand Palace.

Speaking of which, where was the Purple Hand Fort?

Horrid Henry looked around wildly for the fort entrance.

It was gone.

He searched for the Purple Hand throne.

It was gone.

And the Purple Hand cookie tin— GONE!

There was a rustling sound in the shadows. Horrid Henry turned and saw a strange sight.

There was the Purple Hand Fort leaning against the shed.

What?!

Suddenly the fort started moving. Slowly, jerkily, the fort wobbled across the lawn toward the wall on its four new stumpy legs.

Horrid Henry was livid. How dare someone try to steal his fort! This was an outrage. What was the world coming to, when people just sneaked into your

garden and made off with your fort? Well, no way!

Horrid Henry let out a pirate roar.

"RAAAAAAAA!" roared Horrid Henry.

"AHHHHHHH!" shrieked the Fort. CRASH!

The Purple Hand Fort fell to the ground. The raiders ran off, squabbling.

"I told you to hurry, you lazy lump!"

"You're the lazy lump!"

Victory!

Horrid Henry climbed to the top of his fort and grabbed his banner. Waving it proudly, he chanted his victory chant:

NAH NAH NE NAH NAH!

4

HORRID HENRY'S CAR JOURNEY

"Henry! We're waiting!"

"Henry! Get down here!"

"Henry! I'm warning you!"

Horrid Henry sat on his bed and
scowled. His mean, horrible parents
could warn him all they liked. He wasn't
moving.

"Henry! We're going to be late," yelled
Mom.

"Good!" shouted Henry.

"Henry! This is your final warning,"
yelled Dad.

"I don't want to go to Polly's!"
screamed Henry. "I want to go to
Ralph's birthday party."

Mom stomped upstairs.

"Well you can't," said Mom. "You're coming to the christening, and that's that."

"NO!" screeched Henry. "I hate Polly, I hate babies, and I hate you!"

Henry had been a ring bearer at the wedding of his cousin, Prissy Polly, when she'd married Pimply Paul. Now they had a prissy, pimply baby, Vomiting Vera.

Henry had met Vera once before. She'd thrown up all over him. Henry had hoped never to see her again until she was grown up and behind bars, but no such luck. He had to go and watch her be dunked in a vat of water, on the

same day that Ralph was having a
birthday party at Goo-Shooter World.
Henry had been longing for ages to
go to Goo-Shooter World. Today was
his chance. His only chance. But no.
Everything was ruined.

Perfect Peter poked his head around
the door.

"*I'm* all ready, Mom," said Perfect
Peter. His shoes were polished, his
teeth were brushed, and his hair neatly
combed. "I know how annoying it is to
be kept waiting when you're in a rush."

"Thank you, darling Peter," said
Mom. "At least one of my children
knows how to behave."

Horrid Henry roared and attacked. He
was a swooping vulture digging his claws
into a dead mouse.

"AAAAAAAAAEEEEE!" squealed Peter.

"Stop being horrid, Henry!" said Mom.

"No one told me it was today!"
screeched Henry.

"Yes we did," said Mom. "But you weren't paying attention."

"As usual," said Dad.

"*I* knew we were going," said Peter.

"I DON'T WANT TO GO TO POLLY'S!" screamed Henry. "I want to go to Ralph's!"

"Get in the car—NOW!" said Dad.

"Or no TV for a year!" said Mom.

Eeek! Horrid Henry stopped wailing. No TV for a year. Anything was better than that.

Grimly, he stomped down the stairs and out the front door. They wanted him in the car. They'd have him in the car.

"Don't slam the door," said Mom.

SLAM!

Horrid Henry pushed Peter away from the car door and scrambled for the left-hand side behind the driver. Perfect Peter grabbed his legs and tried to climb over him.

Victory! Henry got there first.

Henry liked sitting on the left-hand side so he could watch the speedometer.

Peter liked sitting on the left-hand side so he could watch the speedometer.

"Mom," said Peter. "It's my turn to sit on the left!"

"No it isn't," said Henry. "It's mine."

"Mine!"

"Mine!"

"We haven't even left and already you're fighting?" said Dad.

"You'll take turns," said Mom. "You can switch after we stop."

Vroom. Vroom.

Dad started the car.

The doors locked.

Horrid Henry was trapped.

But wait. Was there a glimmer of hope? Was there a teeny tiny chance? What was it Mom always said when he and Peter were squabbling in the car? "If you don't stop fighting I'm going to turn around and go home!" And wasn't home just exactly where he wanted to be? All he had to do was to do what he did best.

"Could I have a story CD please?" said Perfect Peter.

"No! I want a music CD," said Horrid Henry.

"I want 'Mouse Goes to Town'," said Peter.

"I want 'Driller Cannibals' Greatest Hits'," said Henry.

"Story!"

"Music!"

"Story!"

"Music!"

SMACK!

SMACK!

"Waaaaaa!"

"Stop it, Henry," said Mom.

"Tell Peter to leave me alone!"
screamed Henry.

"Tell Henry to leave *me* alone!"
screamed Peter.

"Leave each other alone," said Mom.
Horrid Henry glared at Perfect Peter.
Perfect Peter glared at Horrid Henry.

Horrid Henry stretched. Slowly,
steadily, centimeter by centimeter, he
spread out into Peter's area.

"Henry's on my side!"

"No I'm not!"

"Henry, leave Peter alone," said Dad.
"I mean it."

"I'm not doing anything," said Henry.
"Are we there yet?"

"No," said Dad.

Thirty seconds passed.

"Are we there yet?" said Horrid Henry.

"No!" said Mom.

"Are we there yet?" said Horrid Henry.

"NO!" screamed Mom and Dad.

"We only left ten minutes ago," said Dad.

Ten minutes! Horrid Henry felt as if they'd been traveling for hours.

"Are we a quarter of the way there yet?"

"NO!"

"Are we halfway there yet?"

"NO!!"

"How much longer until we're halfway there?"

"Stop it, Henry!" screamed Mom.

"You're driving me crazy!" screamed Dad. "Now be quiet and leave us alone."

Henry sighed. Boy, was this boring. Why didn't they have a decent car, with built-in video games, movies, and

jacuzzi? That's just what he'd have, when he was king.

Softly, he started to hum under his breath.

"Henry's humming!"

"Stop being horrid, Henry!"

"I'm not doing anything," protested Henry. He lifted his foot.

"MOM!" squealed Peter. "Henry's kicking me."

"Are you kicking him, Henry?"

"Not yet," muttered Henry. Then he screamed.

"Mom! Peter's looking out of my window!"

"Dad! Henry's looking out of *my* window."

"Peter breathed on me."

"Henry's breathing loud on purpose."

"Henry's staring at me."

"Peter's on my side!"

"Tell him to stop!" screamed Henry and Peter.

Mom's face was red.

Dad's face was red.

"That's it!" screamed Dad.

"I can't take this anymore!" screamed Mom.

Yes! thought Henry. We're going to turn back!

But instead of turning around, the car screeched to a halt at a gas station.

"We're going to take a break," said Mom. She looked exhausted.

"Who needs to pee?" said Dad. He looked even worse.

"Me," said Peter.

"Henry?"

"No," said Henry. He wasn't a baby. He knew when he needed to pee and he didn't need to now.

"This is our only stop, Henry," said Mom. "I think you should go."

"NO!" screamed Henry. Several people looked up. "I'll wait in the car."

Mom and Dad were too tired to argue. They disappeared into the station with Peter.

Rats. Despite his best efforts, it looked like Mom and Dad were going to carry on. Well, if he couldn't make them turn back, maybe he could *delay* them? Somehow? Suddenly Henry had a wonderful, spectacular idea. It couldn't be easier, and it was guaranteed to work. He'd miss the christening!

Mom, Dad, and Peter got back in the car. Mom drove off.

"I need to pee," said Henry.

"Not now, Henry."

"I NEED TO PEE!" screamed Henry. "NOW!"

Mom headed back to the gas station.

Dad and Henry went to the restroom.

"I'll wait for you outside," said Dad. "Hurry up or we'll be late."

Late! What a lovely word.

Henry went into the restroom and locked the door. Then he waited. And waited. And waited.

Finally, he heard Dad's grumpy voice.

"Henry? Have you fallen in?"

Henry rattled the door.

"I'm locked in," said Henry. "The door's stuck. I can't get out."

"Try, Henry," pleaded Dad.

"I have," said Henry. "I guess they'll have to break the door down."

That should take a few hours. He settled himself on the toilet seat and got out a comic.

"Or you could just crawl underneath the partition into the next stall," said Dad.

Aaargghh. Henry could have burst into tears. Wasn't it just his rotten luck to try

to get locked in a restroom that had gaps on the sides? Henry didn't really want to be wriggling around on the cold floor. Sighing, he gave the stall door a tug and opened it.

Horrid Henry sat in silence for the rest of the trip. He was so depressed he didn't even protest when Peter demanded his turn on the left. Plus, he felt car sick.

Henry rolled down his window.

"Mom!" said Peter. "I'm cold."

Dad turned the heat on.

"Having the heat on makes me feel sick," said Henry.

"I'm going to be sick!" whimpered Peter.

"I'm going to be sick," whined Henry.

"But we're almost there," screeched Mom. "Can't you hold on until—"

Bleeeechh.

Peter threw up all over Mom.

Bleeeechhh. Henry threw up all over Dad.

The car pulled into the driveway.

Mom and Dad staggered out of the car to Polly's front door.

"We survived," said Mom, mopping her dress.

"Thank God that's over," said Dad, mopping his shirt.

Horrid Henry scuffed his feet sadly behind them. Despite all his hard work, he'd lost the battle. While Rude

Ralph and Dizzy
Dave and Jolly
Josh were dashing
around spraying
each other with
green goo later this
afternoon he'd be
stuck at a boring
party with lots of grown-ups yak yak
yaking. Oh misery!

Ding dong.

The door opened. It was Prissy Polly.
She was in her bathrobe and slippers. She
carried a stinky, smelly, wailing baby
over her shoulder. Pimply Paul followed.

He was wearing a
filthy T-shirt with
vomit down the
front.

"Eeeek," squeaked
Polly.

Mom tried to look

83

as if she had not been through hell and barely lived to tell the tale.

"We're here!" said Mom brightly. "How's the lovely baby?"

"Too prissy," said Polly.

"Too pimply," said Paul.

Polly and Paul looked at Mom and Dad.

"What are you doing here?" said Polly finally.

"We're here for the christening," said Mom.

"Vera's christening?" said Polly.

"It's *next* weekend," said Paul.

Mom looked like she wanted to sag to the floor.

Dad looked like he wanted to sag beside her.

"We've come on the wrong day?" whispered Mom.

"You mean, we have to go and come back?" whispered Dad.

"Yes," said Polly.

"Oh no," said Mom.

"Oh no," said Dad.

"Bleeech," vomited Vera.

"Eeeek!" wailed Polly. "Gotta go."
She slammed the door.

"You mean, we can go home?" said
Henry. "Now?"

"Yes," whispered Mom.

"Whoopee!" screamed Henry. "Hang
on, Ralph, here I come!"

Horrid Henry's
Family, Friends, and Enemies

Aerobic Al

Anxious Andrew

Aunt Ruby..

Beefy Bert.......................

Bossy Bill..

Brainy Brian

Clever Clare.......................

Dad..

Dizzy Dave.......................

Fiery Fiona

...............Fluffy the cat

Goody-Goody Gordon

Gorgeous Gurinder

......................Grandpa

...............Granny

Great Aunt Greta

Greedy Graham

...............Inky Ian

...........Jazzy Jim

Jolly Josh

Jumpy Jeffrey

Kind Kasim

New Nick

Perfect Peter

Pimply Paul

Prissy Polly

Rabid Rebecca

Rude Ralph

Singing Saraya

Soggy Sid

Sour Susan

Stuck-up Steve

Tidy Ted

Tough Toby

Vain Violet......................................

Vomiting Vera..................

Weepy William..................................

The HORRID HENRY books
by Francesca Simon

Illustrated by Tony Ross
Each book contains four stories

HORRID HENRY

Henry is dragged to dancing class against his will; vies with Moody Margaret to make the yuckiest Glop; goes camping; and tries to be good like Perfect Peter—but not for long.

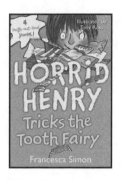

HORRID HENRY TRICKS THE TOOTH FAIRY

Horrid Henry tries to trick the Tooth Fairy into giving him more money; sends Moody Margaret packing; causes his teachers to run screaming from school; and single-handedly wrecks a wedding.

HORRiD HENRY and THE MEGA-MEAN TiME MACHiNE

Horrid Henry reluctantly goes for a hike; builds a time machine and convinces Perfect Peter that boys wear dresses in the future; Perfect Peter plays one of the worst tricks ever on his brother; and Henry's aunt takes the family to a fancy restaurant, so his parents bribe him to behave.

HORRID HENRY'S STINKBOMB

Horrid Henry uses a stinkbomb as a toxic weapon in his long-running war with Moody Margaret; uses all his tricks to win the school reading competition; goes for a sleepover and retreats in horror when he finds that other people's houses aren't always as nice as his own; and has the joy of seeing Miss Battle-Axe in hot water with the principal when he knows it was all his fault.

HORRID HENRY AND THE MUMMY'S CURSE

Horrid Henry indulges his favorite hobby—collecting Gizmos; has a bad time with his spelling homework; starts a rumor that there's a shark in the pool; and spooks Perfect Peter with the mummy's curse.

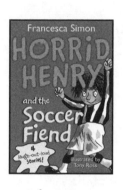

HORRiD HENRY AND THE SOCCER FiEND

Horrid Henry reads Perfect Peter's diary and improves it; goes shopping with Mom and tries to make her buy him some really nice new sneakers; is horrified when his old enemy Bossy Bill turns up at school; and tries by any means, to win the class soccer match.

About the Author

Francesca Simon spent her childhood on the beach in California and then went to Yale and Oxford Universities to study medieval history and literature. She now lives in London with her family. She has written over forty-five books and won the Children's Book of the Year in 2008 at the Galaxy British Book Awards for *Horrid Henry and the Abominable Snowman*.

Photo: Francesco Guidicini

5 9 0 0 0 0 0 0 0

7 8 9 7 0 0